Hi Kids!
I'd like to introduce Watoosi,
a wonderful horse with a great story.
And remember, just like Watoosi,
you are special!

Cowgirl Peg

Belongs To:

To Uzayr-
Cowgirl Peg
Feb. 19, 2010

LIBRARY OF CONGRESS CATALOGING-IN-PUBLICATION DATA
Brown, Corinne.
Wishful Watoosi, the horse that wished he wasn't
p. cm.
ISBN 0-9721057-2-7 HARDCOVER
1. Juvenile Lit 2. Horses 3. Self-esteem 4. Cowgirl Peg 5. Title
I. Corinne Brown II. Character traits; Sundberg, Peggy.
    2005910157
    CIP

First edition printed in Korea by Codra Enterprises, Ltd.

PUBLISHED BY:
Cowgirl Peg Enterprises
P.O. Box 19899, Colorado City, CO 81019
coyotemoonranch@netzero.net
www.cowgrilpeg.com
COPYRIGHT: 2006 © Corinne Brown
DESIGN BY: F + P Graphic Design, Inc.

Wishful Watoosi

The Horse That Wished He Wasn't

Text by Corinne Joy Brown

Edited by Peggy Sundberg

Watercolors by Pat Wiles

When I first came to the Two Bar Ranch, I was six months old and black. My mother was black, too. I never met my Dad.

But soon my coat started to show spots. I looked at myself in the pond. Oh my. They were everywhere.

It didn't take long to find other animals with spots.

Some had spotted noses.

Some had spotted fur

Or spotted scales.

Or spotted skin.

But none were just like me.

At first the spots were very, very small. But by the time I was 2 years old, they were bigger and still everywhere. None of the other horses had them. Why me? I looked like a clown.

One day the big wagon came to town.
We got to watch the parade.

Great horses pulled
the fire wagon and people cheered. Mother was very proud.
She said these were the most important horses in the land.

They had big heads.
Big necks. Big hooves.
But they didn't have spots.

"Look!" I whinnied. "On the back of the fire wagon! There's a dog that's black and white like me! Spots all over." He wore a red collar and barked. Loud!

When the wagon turned
the corner and clattered away,
I knew the truth. Maybe I
wasn't a horse at all.
Maybe I was something else.
But I didn't know what.

I couldn't face the farm anymore.
I couldn't look at myself.
I rolled in the mud
to make the spots go away.

I rolled in the snow, too.

I rolled in the flowers
hoping to cover the spots.
Nothing helped.

I decided not to eat and
maybe the spots would fade.
After three days, I felt sick.
Nothing worked.

On my third birthday
my boy put a red halter
on my head and taught
me to enter a trailer. I had
to walk up and down the
ramp. It was fun.

I liked the trailer.
Once inside, I could hide.
I went in whenever I could.

One Saturday morning my boy announced "This is it. Your big day!"

I didn't know what a "big day" was, but I walked up the ramp and waited. Then I heard the engine growl and away we went. Maybe the time had come to get rid of my spots! Maybe my dreams would come true! When he opened the trailer door and I backed out, we were at the county fair.

I'd never seen so
many horses in my whole life!
Red ones, black ones and
golden ones!
Short ones and tall ones!

Farm horses and
race horses!
But none of them
looked like me.

Then I heard an announcer call my boy's name and a number: "#101".
My boy wore the number on his back. I tasted it but it tasted funny. Away we went.

He led me through a
big gate and into a huge
arena where he walked
me around like a
dog on a leash.
There were other
horses there too – prancing
and showing off. I held
up my head and my nose
turned pink. I was
embarrassed. I didn't look
like them. At the end of the
arena, I saw the giant horses
and their dog waiting to come
out next. The dog jumped from
the wagon. "Psst," he said as we
trotted by. "This is your big day."

Suddenly, we were standing in the middle. The other horses stood there, too. I bowed my head.

"When will this be over?"
I wondered. I wanted to be back home.
The judge walked around and around. I closed my eyes.

My boy took a deep
breath. He patted
my neck. Then the
announcer said
"And the winner is
Number 101 – Watoosi –
a Percheron Appaloosa."
A giant blue ribbon
was fastened on my
halter. My nose
turned pink again.
Was I surprised!
"You are the most
beautiful horse
of all," said
the judge.

My boy gave me a big hug.
"You are special," he said.
"There's no one in the
world like you!"

Corinne Joy Brown with Shamir
(Photo by David Schler)

Watoosi

ABOUT THE AUTHOR

Corinne Joy Brown writes books about Colorado history and the West. But most of all, she likes to write about horses! When she met Watoosi in the summer of 2005 at a barn near Denver, it was love at first sight. He inspired this story and she thanks his owner, Kris Miller, for letting her write about him. She hopes this book will be a fitting tribute to a great horse.

Corinne has a horse of her own named Shamir. He's been her pal for 18 years. Some say he wants to be her next subject! Happy trails! Hope to meet you someday soon.

ABOUT THE ARTIST

Pat Wiles' talents as an illustrator contribute greatly to the Cowgirl Peg books. Her work in *Wishful Watoosi* is awesomely beautiful. Her artwork is her passion, her lifelong dream. Like the author, she understands the need to preserve the Western Heritages that helped build this nation. She cares deeply for the people and animals in her life and enjoys life in the mountains.